James Philip Puglia, Joseph Scott

**The Blue Shop**

Impartial and Humorous Observations on the Life and Adventures of Peter

Porcupine

James Philip Puglia, Joseph Scott

**The Blue Shop**
*Impartial and Humorous Observations on the Life and Adventures of Peter Porcupine*

ISBN/EAN: 9783337306687

Printed in Europe, USA, Canada, Australia, Japan

Cover: Foto ©Raphael Reischuk / pixelio.de

More available books at **www.hansebooks.com**

# THE

# BLUE SHOP

O R

IMPARTIAL AND HUMOROUS OBSERVATIONS

ON THE

## LIFE AND ADVENTURES

O F

# PETER PORCUPINE,

WITH THE

*REAL MOTIVES WHICH GAVE RISE TO HIS*
*ABUSE OF OUR DISTINGUISHED*
*PATRIOTIC CHARACTERS;*

TOGETHER WITH

A FULL AND FAIR REVIEW OF HIS LATE

## SCARE-CROW.

---

BY JAMES QUICKSILVER.

---

### PHILADELPHIA:

Printed by MOREAU DE ST-MÉRY, N° 84. Corner of
Front and Walnut Streets.

August 1796.

# PREFACE.

I T has long been reported, to my knowledge, that the famous life of Peter Porcupine was to be ushered to the public, and this rumour has prevailed so long that it is probable he has begun the interesting history a considerable time ago : his hint relative to such a great undertaking will justify the probability (\*). The term *Parturient Montes* made me expect a volume equal to the importance of the subject. On the 8th. instant, casually looking over Claypoole's paper, I read the advertisement of its publication, and to such a degree was my curiosity excited on the occasion, that I took to my heels in order to procure a copy : I remember, I ran as fast as I could to the *Blue Shop*, but I ran with anxious speed, left the whole first edition should be bought up. My apprehensions however were soon removed : I did not meet the croud, presented to imagination's view, purchasing with

---

(\*) See Life of P. Porcup. Preface, page vij ad med,

avidity that valuable production, perhaps on account of my early attendance, and as foon as I
afked for the edition, a *fmall* pamphlet was han-
ded to me. I thought at firft that he took me
for fome *bigot* to the *Bone to gnaw*, but my fur-
prife was foon over when I heard his kind apof-
trophe. — " This is my life, good man, (exclai-
" med he) it is very cheap, I fell it at the low
" price of *five five-penny-bits*, and on perufing it,
" you will find excellent inftruction conveyed
" through the whole that may tend to *make your*
" *fortune* „. The repetition of the terms *good*
*man* echoed in my ears, was fomething fimilar to
thofe fignificant monofyllabes *my lad*, uttered by
Mathew Carey to Porcupine (\*) whofe life had
I not read, my remarks, perhaps, would be equally poignant. I never knew Porcupine before,
yet he appeared to me as merry and jocular as if
he never had received a fingle line in the epifto-
lary cut-throat ftyle fince he was a baby. His
peculiar magnanimity was then concealed from
me, and to this myftery alone I afcribe my fufpi-
cion of his making fun of my natural fimplicity.
The expreffion " *To make my fortune* " made me
think lightly of the price of the pamphlet,
which I readily paid for, and proceeded with ea-
ger fteps to my garret, full of curiofity to come
at fo *valuable a fecret*.

My Reader muft neceffarily be informed that

---

(\*) See page 37, in fin.

no man can be more induftrious than I am, yet in fpite of all my corporeal and fpiritual exertions, I find myfelf for ever in arrears. The more I feek the blind Goddefs Fortune, the more weary and poor I become in purfuing the Jilt, and inftead of heaping up dollars in a worfted ftocking, which I keep for the purpofe, half-worn Englifh and American *Coppers* form the bulk of my earthly treafure. Labouring under this inceffant fatigue I look older by half than I am, — nay — every time my barber fhaves me, endeavouring to poife his razor with trembling hand, he looks aghaft on my care-worn vifage, and with accents expreffive of his feelings, afks me if I am fick. It muft be fo indeed when a hair - dreffer difcovers fymptoms, that the well-known *Doctor Sangredo* could hardly trace. Am I then blameable for my endeavours to acquire an eafy fortune, and cheer my drooping fpirits, or would not my Reader, were he in my fituation, profit by fuch a beneficial *Lapis Philofophorum*? Let him not therefore be furprifed if I flipped into *Porcupine's* hands fifty fix Jerfey pennies, for, the fpeculation was founded on folid arithmetical principles, and were Squire *Holland* (*) himfelf here, he would think me worthy of the honour of being his underftrapper.

On reading the Title of the darling Publication, I found myfelf ftrongly prepoffeffed in its

---

(*) An Attorney once mafter of P. Porcup. See pag. 22 and 23.

favor, and fervently difpofed to an inftant perufal of the whole. — My dull capacity did not at firft permit me to tafte its beauties, nor enable me to penetrate into the receffes of the main object which was the *fure and infallible guide for enterprizing young men who wifh to make a fortune by writing Pamphlets*; I was therefore obliged to go over it again. — Though the fecret is only applicable to young men, and not to old Batchelors, I was, by no means, difcouraged from entering on a fecond reading; and at length I came to know that a fortune may be eafily made by any Author, who creeps into the good graces of that *generous* printer Thomas Bradford.—I never knew he was fo *kind* a patron to original writers, as Porcupine defcribes him, and indeed were I not actually engaged, I would think myfelf happy to employ him. — What emoluments could I expect, and be almoft fure of, from this publication if paffing through the channel of his *liberal* prefs! I muft poftpone his Eulogium to a further period, and at prefent I beg leave only in this public manner to exprefs thofe ardent hopes I feel, of making a rapid fortune. — I am determined, notwithftanding my bald pate, to try Peter's *fecret*, and will adhere to it, until I, like another *Chevalier d'induftrie,* can fcrape as much from the favings of rigid œconomy as will enable me alfo to fet up a ftationer's fhop. Nothing is difficult to a perfevering man, and though I have not even a *private's-pay* to expend for a *fubfcription* to a *circulating library,* I will fcribble away as faft as I can, in order to lodge fome *five-penny-bits*, where farthings only were depofited. This is my chief aim, and I now truft that fuch franknefs and fincerity will merit your patronage. — Is there any better *little plain Englifh* than this, or did you ever before hear any Author thus publicly make fo candid a confeffion ? — I am already too old to impofe on you, and Porcupine, I affure you, is but a *Lad* if compared to me.

But let me not forget the bufinefs I am about.— No production, of all thofe publifhed by Peter, has, I ingenuoufly own it, appeared to me more witty, fcientific and fafhionable than his Life, and anxious to pay him that homage which an exalted genius juftly deferves, I have undertaken a fort of review of his diftinguifhed performance. — I do not wifh to deal in the prolixity of panegyric, but rather relate a concife unvarnifhed tale.

I never cut any throat in my life except that of a bottle of claret, when I had no cork-fcrew, but at the fame time I would not fubmit to the *fufpenfion* of the *habeas corpus*, and the *abolition* of focieties. It is as cruel to cut human throats as to divide mankind by unlinking the chain that connects them and fcattering them through the World, like heaps of hay o'er the autumnal field. You will fee no extremes of this kind in my remarks, nor *Roafter*, nor even *Scare-Crow* defcend from my garret, for I do not like to terrify any animal, nor do I wifh to burn my fingers at a hot fire. — To fum up the whole in a few words, my real intentions are to beftow impartial

praifes on the merits of Peter Porcupine, to gra-
tify the laudable curiofity of the Reader, and to
lay the foundation of my future fortune, if the
American Character retains its wonted generofity.

THE

# THE

# BLUE SHOP

### OR

## IMPARTIAL AND HUMOROUS OBSERVATIONS

#### ON THE

## LIFE AND ADVENTURES

#### OF

# PETER PORCUPINE, &c.

IF to be defcended from an illuftrious family reflects honor on any man, as Porcupine judicioufly obferves (1), it is certainly a pity that he fhould have been born in a *cottage* with two windows only, and that he fhould be the humble fon of an obfcure, mulifh farmer.

His elevated genius would, I dare fay, render him capable of fwaying the regal fcepter, had not ungrateful nature refufed to puff his foul into

---

(1)-See his Life, page 9.

A

the body of his Royal Highnefs the prince ef
Wales; but fuch is the lot of the moft emi-
nent Authors, whofe abilities fpring from neceffity it felf, and are fharpened on the grindftone
of diftrefs. I agree with him entirely in opinion
that his mean birth is a great honour to him,
and would appear ftill greater had he humbled
himfelf lower than his ftory relates his condi-
tion, for, his plain fare or the *æconomical fire* and
*candles ufed by his mother* will never be any dif-
grace to him in the opinion of a difcerning
Reader, who confiders the fimple tale as matter
of fact.

His voluntary renunciation to all kind of
nobility whatfoever, fhews plainly that *he tells
the naked truth*, without *defcending to the mifera-
ble fhifts of Doctor Franklin* (1). It is however
furprifing to me how a man of fuch candor
fhould endeavour to impofe himfelf as a Baronet on a *certain young Lady in London*, during
his three months revelling there. I never be-
lieved fuch a report, though it came from a
refpectable quarter; becaufe he made no mention
of it — His former familiarity with Colonel
Debieg, and his tranfactions with Lord Edward
Fitzgerald and General Frederick might have
eafily flattered his juvenile enterprifes, but I
am fure he would not have diffembled his foibles
had he been really guilty of them. — The fact
is, that his adventures there, were paffed over
in filence, becaufe bufinefs of *courtfhip* is more

(1) Page 10, ad med.

agreeably tranfacted than related (1). I admire
his delicacy on the occafion.

But, to return to Doctor Franklin, Porcupine
feems too inexorable to *dead* men. I would not
be a corpfe ftretched on a field of battle, and
met by fuch a ferocious Britifh Lyon for all the
pennies and five-penny-bits that Authors of
pamphlets have gained fince the profeffion of
fcribbling was inftituted; for I do believe that
the *fergeant major* would level me with his
mufket firft, and hackle me in fuch a manner
with his long fword afterwards, that I fhould be
provoked to rife up on my ftiff underftanders,
and give him the dead man's pinch as a token
of remembrance.

It is indeed a great advantage to attack a
man of inferior force, but it is greater undoubtedly to infult a character from whom no reta-
liation is dreaded. I muft be indulged with
the liberty of introducing one of his expref-
fions before hand, and I hope the Reader will
have no objections, becaufe I think it adapted
to our prefent fubject.

Porcupine fays in page 20 of his life, that
*on the 6th May* 1783, *he like Don Quixote fallied
forth to feek adventures.* — Now I think his
comparifon too exaggerated—Did Don Quixote
fuppofe that by attacking the wind-mills, no
Giant would refent the infult and come forward?
Certainly not, for, though he had no enemies

(1) See pag. 31. *How thefe three months were employed it is not neceffary to fay here.........* The Ladies
*will, &c.....*

. A 2

in the action, yet he thought there were some. If Porcupine thinks it worth while for the fake of inftruction to read over again the *ftory* and *burial of Grifoftcmo*, I am fure he will find, that Don Quixote fpoke in a proud and fevere tone to the ftandersby who wanted to follow the *beautiful Marcela*, but never faid any thing againt the corpfe, either before or after its burial (1). Now, is this the way to feek for adventures like Don Quixote, or is the criticifm on Doctor Franklin's character to be thought a glorious topic in a military Author, who writes his own Life ? Don Quixote was crazy, but generous at the fame time — Does Porcurpine renounce his claim to generofity, becaufe he fuppofes himfelf to be fober ? I wifh he would follow his adopted example, or elfe I muft infift on his renouncing the glory of having come to America *like Don Quixote*, for it is fcandalous to boaft one thing, and do another.

If Porcupine fpeaks ill of Doctor Franklin, becaufe he is dead, what would he fay of General Wafhington were he not alive ? The fact is, that the Doctor can be no more of fervice to his Country, nor was he in a fituation at the time our Adventurer appeared on this fhore to *write* him any compliment, either in the courtezan ftyle or otherwife. I muft now refign this fubject, for it looks like affectation to fwell up a pamphlet with digreffions againft the manes of any man.

---

(1) The Life and Advent. of Don Quixote by Michael Cervantes Saavedra.

( 13 )

Whether *a damfon tree, or a clump of filberts fhaded one window* (1), or whether a hill of dung (the ufual merchandize of farmers) ftopped both, it is not in my opinion an object deferving the attention of a witty writer. — Why fhould I ef-patiate on the popularity of *a man driving a plough for two pence a day,* or *furveying the lands* (2) of two contending ruftics, and what is ftill of lefs confequence, why fhould I dwell on the number of the *legitimate* brothers of our Porcupine, their *age* and *profeffion* ? (3)—No, no.— It feems to me that the Reader is pleafed at my declining the fuperficial tafk, for, whether *Meffieurs Porcupines* have been reared in rural obfcurity, or paffed their days in *military idlenefs,* it is a matter which little contributes to amufe our citizens, and much lefs to excite the compaffion of the Federal Government in favour of our fhop-keeper.

It is equally improper to confume time with a defcription of the capers of his youth, by taking notice of the various fchemes that between the fifteenth and feventeenth year of his age were concerted by him — In candor, however, I muft obferve that (aftonifhing as it may appear) a poor, neglected, and worfe educated farmer's boy fhould *ex motu proprio* think on high life, on the *wooden walls of England* (4), on the victories of that nation over the French, Spaniards, Turks, Chinefe, and all mankind put together ; yet this fellow had a greater idea than any Englifh warrior

(1) See pag. 10 in princip. ‖ (3) See pag. 12 ad med..
(2) See pag. 11 in fin. ‖ (4) See pag. 17 in fin.

was ever capable of conceiving. — He even defpifed his powerful mother Country, for, though he felt *emboldened* at her *glory* (1), and equally anxious to *contribute* by every means in his power to the national grandeur, he thought fhe was *too fmall a compafs for him* (2) — I wonder that *Captain George Berkley, brother to the Earl, and commander of the Pegafus man of war at Spithead* (3) did not humble the pride of a beardlefs cow-driver, for undervaluing that very fpot, where fo many Admirals, Lords, and the grand Auguft family of the Royal Guelphs have placed their refidence.—I might from the extreme forbearance of that Right Honourable failor, infer that he had a very flight *point d'honneur* for his profeffion and Country, becaufe, were he truly martial, he would have immediately correfted the impertinence of this forward lad, by a gentle flagellation from *Mifs Roper*'s hand (4); perhaps, however, M. Berkley through his extreme veneration for the charafter of an Englifhman, looked upon the prefumption of young Peter as the youthful glow of future greatnefs : but alas ! Porcupine did not profit by this indulgence, for, his magnanimity was foon at an end. When he found himfelf in the captain's prefence, he tells us, that he looked *confufed* and *blufhed* (5) — Is it not a droll fcene to fee fuch a promifing boy take a boat, go on board a King's fhip, requeft

---

(1) See pag. 17 in fin.  ||  (4) See pag. 19 in princip.
(2) See pag. 20 in princip. ||  (5) See ibid. ad med.
(3) See pag. 18 in fin.  ||

an audience with the commander, and prove himſelf a awkward youth after all ?

Yes, the whole formidable fleet at Spithead, unrivalled England, the fertile kingdom of Scotland, and the populous country of Ireland, were at that time a mere mouſe to him. — He looked upon Great Britain as an indiviſible geometrical point, and notwithſtanding his being born in a little cottage with two windows only, he calls that glorious and productive Iſland *little*, even before he travelled through it, that is to ſay *inſigni-ficant* and *deſpicable*. — There is a fine geographer for you, a generous Engliſhman, and a faithful vaſſal to the King his ſovereign Lord and Maſter ! ! !

Our youth thus taken up with his great projects, and at laſt determined to put them into execution began to diſregard *the ſinging of the birds, the cry of the hounds,* and every other rural pleaſure : he alſo neglected *to weed the wheat, to lead a ſingle horſe* to eat *the barley,* and having jumped over the fences *quitted* the farm, *perhaps, for ever* (1)—At this moment, probably, Don Quixote came to his mind, whoſe adventures, I ſuppoſe, he had read and got by heart, while he *was driving the ſmall birds from the turnip ſeed, and the rooks from the peas* (2)-I declare that his ambition to imitate ſuch a knight errant puzzles me exceedingly, but I ſhall not detain my Reader with further remarks on ſuch a droll vagary in our Pet.

---

(1) See pag. 20 ad med. || (2) See pag. 12 infin.

In all likelihood, his father was not pleafed at his departure, becaufe he was deprived of a fon, *who did as much work as three men in the parifh of Farnham* (1). Unfortunate *honeft pride* to be thus checked by a fpoiled Youth! Yet the Reader ought to paufe on the motives, that forced Porcupine to *figh for a fight of the World* (2), before he pronounces judgment on his difobedience — Pet was, I believe, as fenfible then, as he feems to be now, and he confidered his father's boafting of his manual labor as a fort of humiliation.—" What! (faid he, while he was *dafhing through the brakes and coppices* (3)). ,, I am here like a mere jack afs, which is fit ,, for no other purpofe than hard work and drud- ,, gery! Was I born to *drive the team and hold* ,, *the plough ?* (4). Away with fuch rufticity ,, and fevere toil. — I will foon change profef- ,, fions. — I know how to read and write, and ,, fhall, therefore, figure in the world, which cer- ,, tainly ftands in need of my abilities. " — Had the old farmer known the clandeftine revolution of Pet, I dare fay, he would have fhut him up in the cottage, and mortify him by bringing one of the other boys along with him to the *Hop-Fair at Wey-Hill*; but the father was too ftupid to take the hint, and thus loft him for ever.

He faw *the ftage-coach rattling down*, *up he got, went to London* (5), found himfelf after having *paid his fare at Ludgate-Hill* with only

---

(1) See pag. 13 ad med.
(2) See pag. 20 in princip.
(3) See pag. 20 ad med.

(4) See pag. 13 in princip.
19 in fin.
(5) See pag. 20 in fin.

*half*

*half a crown in* his *pocket* ( 1 ). He happens to creep into the good graces of a certain gentleman there — Mr. Holland the *Attorney* cafually called on him, and Porcupine was employed. We now fee after fo many adventures our promifing genius *perched 'upon a high ftool* (2), and furnifhed with the beft opportunities of exercifing his talents, and rapidly improving under the wholefome inftructions of an elderly *Laundrefs* (3).

Arrived thus far, I cannot help difapproving altogether the notice, which Porcupine too frequently takes of John Swanwick — In one refpect I look upon his criticifm to be in earneft; but, if fo, why fhould Mr. Swanwick be the topic of his animadverfion merely for having difmiffed him from employment? Had he not a right to chufe another copyift of his poems, when the abilities of Porcupine did not anfwer his expectations? Does our writer forget, that he plainly confeffed his *ignorance of the rules of Grammar,* and *his many miftakes in copying?* (4). — No body will difpute that *he wrote out two or three times the whole Englifh grammar,* and *got it by heart* at laft while pofted as *fentinel,* and that he *acquired the little learning of which he is mafter* (5); Yet it muft be obferved that *Lowth's grammar* contains no rule for refined poetry, and this was precifely the object for which Mr. Swanwick wanted Porcupine; but as *a clever worfted knot upon his fhoulders* (6) cannot make him fuffi-

---

(1) See pag. 21 in princ.  ‖  (4) See pag. 26 ad med.
(2) See pag. 22 ad med.  ‖  (5) See pag. 27 ad med,
(3) See pag. 23 in fin.  ‖  (6) See ibid. in fin,

ciently converfant in fuch kind of works, he
fhould have concealed the difappointment and
make no more noife about it. Were Mr. Swanwick of a bilious conftitution, and determined to
retort the cenfures of Peter Porcupine (on
fuppofing them to be meant in earneft), he might
call the Author of the TUTEUR ANGLAIS a true
impoftor, for having made himfelf the *Author*
of a grammar, which, though a wretched one,
can by no means be the production of his genius,
and who would not be of the fame opinion, after
the perufal of his life page 33, in which his
imperfect knowledge of the French language,
on account of his very fhort ftay in France, is
plainly declared ?

While on the other hand I intend to do juftice
to the great penetration of Peter Porcupine, by
confidering his ftrictures as ironical, I cannot
agree with him in making Mr. Swanwick the
fport of his lively wit for the fake of public
humour. I do not difcover any *military* generofity in that giant, who fpends his time in ridi-
culing a pigmy — In whatever light the difpro-
portion may be viewed, I mean only the vifible
and corporeal, for we know that Porcupine as
a grenadier may fall into the ranks, whereas
Swanwick is fcarcely fit for a drummer — If any
controverfy in point of talents does not take
place between the two rivals, I am convinced
that none will in point of ftature, or englifh
*bruifing.*

I cannot, however, pafs un noticed Peter's GAR-
ÇON FENDU (1), an exceeding funny expreffion,

---

(1) See pag. 31 ad med.

which, notwithstanding my usual gravity, made me almost split my sides laughing — " Dang ,, my buttons (exclaimed I) but this writer is ,, mighty witty, and a good privateer too (though ,, married) on the coasts of *Irish-Town* " ; and indeed I was not mistaken in my conjecture, for I remember, that when he was seeking a harbour for Mr. Holland's *Laundress*, in order to save such *beauty* from shipwreck , he piloted her into one of the Havens on those happy Shores. If the Reader takes the trouble of perusing the 23d. page, he will find that I refer to his own expressions.

A principal objection, however, I must make to his charitable intention of conferring the office of Abbess on the said Laundress, and this is, that she being *the oldest, and ugliest of the officious sisterhood,* will never be able to obtain the vote of the Nuns consistorum.

The taste of such Convents is more refined than Porcupine supposes — Beauty is the greatest prerogative considered among them, whether *young*, or *old*. — Though I am convinced that he has a perfect knowledge of the constitution and bye-laws of that society, I shall in a few words make a distinction, in order to render the meaning more clear to him. — By *young* are signified those innocent girls, who zealous in sacrificing to Venus, enter the Noviciate on tryal, and if approved, endeavour to procure an honest genteel living by their nightly devotion to that goddess — By the *old* we conceive those, who, in spite of the wrecks, of time, endeavour to re-animate declining beauty, by the effacious influence of peculiar waters, paints, patches and perfumes, and thus retain as it were some appearance of priftine grandeur in the midft of ruins.

I am well affured then from Porcupine's own defcription, that Mr. Holland's *Laundrefs* could never obtain a fixed refidence in the temple of Beauty, and, of courfe, he will have no objections, I hope, to defift from procuring his old acquaintance a fituation. But to return to the *Garçon fendu*, I would be curious enough to know the true meaning of it, for I apprehend I fhall differ from Peter in his idea of it — I know the French language as thoroughly as he does, without leffening his merit as a teacher, and as to the term *fendu* I think it means in Englifh *wounded*. Now, I conceive, that, as *fighting* is more the province of a *military* man than that of a *trading* citizen, I think it is a bufinefs more fuitable to Porcupine than to Mr. Swanwick, who, I guefs, never carried *brown befs* on his fhoulders in his life — The author of the foregoing term will at any rate, hereafter, throw light on his ambiguous epithet by a copious explanation of it, if the bufinefs of the fhop permits him.

We left our *underftrapping Quill-driver* at Mr. Holland's *obfcure* office *in Gray's Inn* (1), we muft, therefore, fuffer him to efcape, in order to breathe the frefh air — The arrangement of his hiftory, of which he himfelf is the hero and the writer, is not very exact, yet I fhall proceed in fuch order as his intricate adventures may allow. The bufinefs of an Attorney did not furnifh his mind with fufficient entertainment, and informa-

---

(1) See pag. 22 ad med.

tion. A profeſſion of a more active and manly kind was ſought for by him, and the military ſervice, of courſe, at firſt attracted his attention — He ran away to Chatham and enliſted; remained a whole year as ſentinel (here was an ample field for his enterpriſing genius ! ! !); embarked with his regiment, and arrived at Nova Scotia, where he employed *Squires* in his ſervice to *bring him a glaſs of grog, and take care of his knapſack* (1) Who would believe ſuch extravagant adventures, were not Porcupine himſelf the author, the contriver and hiſtorian at the ſame time ? In the courſe of ſome time the caſe was altered. Our ſoldier was obliged to part with his reputable retinue, for, *the regiment being relieved, was ſent home* (1).

What a change from having *Squires* for his attendants, and be after obliged to waſh and mend his own ſhirt and ſtockings, poliſh his ſhoes, and even comb, greaſe and ſhake flour on his head of hair, and whiſkers ! ! ! But ſuch are the viciſſitudes of the ſons of Mars. Had he never experienced the meanneſs and poverty of a ſoldier, he would have taken no notice of his *ordering a ſquire to bring him a glaſs of grog* — What a difference, however, between him and his father ! The old farmer contended himſelf with an humble *pot of ale* (2); but Porcupine thought it too poor for his conſtitution — The king's pay could afford ſome heart cheering liquor.

He landed at Portſmouth, and forty ſix days after obtained his diſcharge from THE RIGHT

---

(1) See page 28 in fin. ‖ (2) See page 14 in fin.

HONOURABLE MAJOR LORD EDWARD FITZ-
GERALD, COMMANDING HIS MAJESTY'S 54th
REGIMENT OF FOOT, WHEREOF LIEUTENANT
GENERAL FREDERICK IS COLONEL.

Honourable certificates ! I wonder how fuch
great characters, who are commonly employed
in vifiting the ladies, going to plays, and procuring pimps, panders and procureffes on certain
occafions, I wonder, I fay, how they could attend to fuch elegant and well written certificates,
as thofe publifhed by Porcupine in favour of
William Cobbett — Some fmart fecretary equal
in abilities to our Author was then employed, I
fhould fuppofe for this purpofe, as the aforefaid
gentlemen, I am perfuaded, never took any pains
in getting lowth's grammar by heart. But be it as
it may, his character is immaculate to the very
day of his difcharge, and no body can fay peas
to it.

Now, ye *monftrous, diforganiziug, democratic
gang,* what do you fay to fuch documents ? They
are *printed,* you fee — Will you doubt their
exiftence ? Will you dare to deny their authen-
ticity, when Porcupine folemnly declares *himfelf
to be in poffeffion of incontrovertible proofs,* that fuch
documents were once iffued ? Whether they were
granted to William Cobbet, Peter Porcupine, or
old Carlifle, or whether William Cobbett is the
*real* or *fictitious* name of the poffeffor, it is not
your province to know — You have no other
right than that of believing and holding your
peace — That's what I earneftly recommend
you to do, if you wifh to avoid a future fcourging
from our Hiftorian.

On taking a view of the account he gives of

his life, fince his *difmiffion* from the militar·
fervice of king George the III, a great omiffion
appears to have been made by him in totally
forgetting his three months career in London;
fo that we cannot trace a fingle veftige of his
various chara&ers on that great theatre —
I confefs, in fpite of my penetrating properties as
real *Quickfilver*, I find barriers to every channel
of information: recolle& Reader, however, what
I mentioned in the beginning of thefe *Obferva-*
*tions* (page 10). Take the hint, and have patience
for a little while; you will fee fhortly that all
will come to light, and, that time, that great
Revealer of humain affairs, will foon let the cat
out of the bag, and make you acquainted with
the adventures, courtfhip &c. of a *certain pre-*
*tended Baronet*, which at prefent I cannot indulge
you with, till I finifh the life of Porcupine.

*But before I go any further* (I ufe his own
elegant phrafeology in page 31 ad med.), *it feems*
*neceffary to fay a word or two about*. FRENCH
LEAVE......... What fhall I fay? By George
I fwear, I know not what to fay — I wifh I had
not introduced his *phrafeology*, for I am fick of
it already — It would be better to defcend to
the fhifts of Do&or Franklin and fneak off in
time, before the *parifian ftorm gathers*(1)..... But I
am engaged like Porcupine, when *he found himfelf*
*before the captain of a marching Regiment*, infor-
ming us that *there was no retreating* (2) —This
is the devil down right— Curious Reader, I am

---

(1). See page 33 in fin.  ‖  (2). See page 24 in fin.

well aware you would wish to have my opinion on the terms *French Leave*, but cannot I scratch my head and rub my eyes a little before I advance it? — Attend, if you please — As a proof of my being averse to prolixity and thinking too highly of my own opinion, I shall give it to you in a few words, provided you dont laugh — The copious wit and long winded argumentation, Porcupine has displayed in his cursory remarks on the above expression, are so brilliant and profound that neither I, nor, I believe, any body else CAN CLEARLY COMPREHEND THEM — This is the whole mystery revealed—Can I say more? I hope you will not think me too laconic on the occasion.

Having thus *extricated* myself *from this bobble*, without, I hope, disappointing your expectations, I shall pursue my observations in as chearful and blithe a mood as that of the whistling plough-boy, who earns but *two pence* sterling *per diem* (1).

It is somewhat strange, that Peter Porcupine after having been so exceedingly minute in the *history* of his youth, the *description* of his paternal cottage, the *politics* of his father, the *employments* of his brothers, his *scaring* the crows, his *running away* to London, his *situation* with Mr Holland, the *Laudress, certificates,* and several other *interesting* matters, which he has so happily enumerated, should be so remiss as to give no account How HIS SUDDEN fortune was acquired, which enabled him to make such an expensive

_____

(1) See pag. 11 in fin.

tour, immediately after his military difcharge—
He tells us that he went to France, paffed over
to Holland (where he obtained the recommen-
datory letter from the American Ambaffador at
the Hague to Mr. Jefferfon), returned to France and *had actually hired a coach* to go to
Paris (1) — Now it is well known that coach-
hire is very dear in France, on account of the
fcarcity of horfes occafioned by the great de-
mand of the french cavalry; of courfe a tra-
veller in thofe countries muft have a heavier
purfe to travel in fuch a ftyle than a *difmiffed*
fergeant could be fuppofed to poffefs — The
fact is, however, that Porcupine put on the
affected airs of a Gentleman and *actually hired
the coach*; but by what well-concerted project
he avoided the expence of coach-hire, is a
fecret beft known to himfelf alone, and equal,
perhaps, to thofe he practifed in his midnight
perambulations through the *precincts of St. Giles*,
London — But he prudently throws a deep
veil over all his nocturnal fcenes in that quarter, which the moft quick-fighted of the bloody
Democrats could by no means penetrate —
Had not I, or fome body elfe read his *honourable difcharge* from Lord Fitzgerald (2), and
the very *diftinguifhed thanks* returned him by
General Frederick (3), fome *fufpicions* againft
his character might be eafily entertained; but
notwithftanding their *plaufibility*, his authentic
documents muft wafh away every afperfion and

---

(1) See pag. 34 in princip. ‖ (3) See pag. 30 in princip.
(2) See pag. 29 ad med. ‖

C

enfure him the good opinion of his Readers.

I have touched on this point to *fruftrate* the mifreprefentations of our unmerciful cut-throat Jacobins, and ſhield his *ſpotleſs* fame from the poniard of calumny.

With the anſwer of Mr. Jefferſon to our adventurer (1) (which for the ſake of huſhing the noiſy tongues of our ſans-culottes, I expect he is in poſſeſſion of) we ſee him wafted over the wide Atlantic to the United States of America — Will our *peſtilential Democratic club Room* have any objection to his character ſince his diſcharge from the Britiſh ſervice and his appearance in this Country? Prudence directs me not to ſtem the impetuous torrent of American Jacobiniſm, but I would adviſe them to be cautions in their attacks when I can aſſure them that Porcupine has brought a letter from HIS EXCELLENCY our Ambaſſador at the Hague, and they muſt, I expect it, be on their guard or abide by the conſequence.

I am extremly pleaſed at the proper correction our admired Author gives Doctor Prieſtley— If a Batchelor can be indulged for ſome human foibles, I muſt expreſs my hatred againſt that old Gentleman — An Engliſhman who delights in the ruin of his *glorious* Country, and prefers the title of a Citizen of the United States to that of a loyal vaſſal to his Moſt Excellent Majeſty George the third, is undoubtedly a HYPOCRITE — A preacher who denies that *One* can be *Three*, and of courſe

(1) See page 35.

that *Three* can be One, is a *philosopher* of the
moft *abominable* principles, and knows nothing
about *fyllogiftical* forms of reafoning — I agree
with Porcupine that the Americans at his arrival on their fhores have received him with
loud acclamations and every demonftration of
joy ; and after all they have acquired in this old
*chymift* a very fo fo, and dangerous citizen, for
I have always execrated his very name, fpecta-
cles, fermons, and even his mode of delivering
them — Now I perceive, this Porcupine has
more docility than I have — His enmity is not
fo *inveterate*, tho' mine arifes from principles,
and his from *cafualty* ; and his mild conduct
while a private and corporal, fhews a generous
heart incapable of harbouring an old grudge—
He was a friend to the Doctor, unknown to
him at his arrival in New-York, but the im-
prudence or rather thoughtlefs conduct of the
*french Delegate* was not approved by our adventurer. Prieftley did not receive his countryman
in the manner he expected, which in all likelihood gave rife to the fcribbling we have fo
often feen publifhed — Kind Reader, conceive,
if you pleafe, a better opinion of Porcupine in
this refpect, for, had you been in his place you
would have thought the *Obfervations on Doctor
Prieftley's Emigration* too infufficient fatisfaction
for the above contempt — I might apply on this
occafion to the philofopher the exclamation
made ufe of by the *Irifh Captain* to Porcupine,
when he enlifted; *By Jafes, my lad, and you have
had a narrow efcape* (1) !

---

(1) See page 25 in princip.

An intimate friend of mine ſtanding by me, who is a handſome Beau, intreats me this moment to take ſome notice of the *literary* merit of Mrs. Rowſon — His recommendation in favour of that lady ſeems to me ſome what partial; but who is ſhe? Is ſhe any inſulted member of Con-greſs, or diſtinguiſhed *patriotic* character? No, ſhe is a woman, and all women are commonly Ariſtocrats — This is one of the twelve rea-ſons for wich I am a Batchelor; but, (ſays the complaiſant youth) " ſhe has compoſed the *famous* " production entitled the *Fille de Chambre* " — What is that to me? — It is as eaſy to compoſe a volume for a *fille de chambre* alone, as for twenty old virgins together — I cannot comply with the requeſt, for, I would not wiſh my Reader ſhould think that I court the attention of the ariſtocratic female beauties. Mr. SNUB a warm votary to her merits, took much pains to defend them at the time of the yellow fever, and that will do, I gueſs; his defence, however, was a little in the blackguard ſtyle, and ill-ſuited to that melancholy period of tears and mourning — Porcupine, I beg you will keep your temper — I do not mean to reproach you for your imprudent attack on the abilities of that lady, though you richly deſerve it — Your conduct is the more cenſurable as you have been profeſſedly an admirer of the fair ſex — Witneſs this ye London belles!

But to return to more important ſubjects — We now enter into the authoring buſineſs of Porcupine, or rather his tranſactions with our Bookſellers who, according to his expreſſion, (1) *are in general a cruel race.*

─────────────────────────

(1) See pag. 47 ad med.

If ever I miftrufted any printer or Bookfeller (for this is not the firft, nor the fecond, nor even the third work I am author of ), it has been Mathew Carey — He is an Irifhman and acquainted with all the advantages a printer may take of authors, almoft fince his cradle — Had Porcupine dealt with him at firft, he would not have made fuch a rapid fortune as he did by Thomas Bradford — Carey is an author himfelf, and an artful one too — Above all, he is the proudeft Ariftocrat, and the moft uncivil of all his breathen whom I know. — What! to dub a gentleman ftranger, who *had on his back a coat as good as* his, and the whole tribe of printers(1)with the humiliating title of MY LAD (2)! Did any of my Readers ever hear fuch impertinence offered to an author of merit, refpect and credit? The prudence of Porcupine in taking no notice of a ftationer's hauteur deferves applaufe, and greater is ftill due to him for mentioning the name of Mathew Carey with a kind of refpect — The *fear* of meeting a match in Saint Mathew, may, it is true, be confidered as the *caufe* of moderation in Saint Peter — He knows that a controverfy among Authors is neither an honour nor improvement to literature, and his refentment on the foregoing occafion, in particular, might hurry him into inextricable difficulties — Who could fuppofe that Porcupine, fo fevere a foe to his adverfaries, would decline a literary combat with Mathew Carey, were it not for prudential motives?

---

(1). See pag. 42 ad med. || (2) See pag. 37 in fin,

Having occasionally mentioned Mr. Bradford, I recollect some observations from the
preface, which it were an injustice to him to
omit — The good opinion I entertain of this
sincere republican proceeds from the knowledge
I have of his accuracy in printing both in the
*English, French, Spanish and Italian languages*, in
which he so much excells all the other printers
of Philadelphia, without diminishing the tranf-
cendant merit of our great paper-fpoiler Mr.
Benjamin Davis, whose person I respect so
much, that I would not, for any confideration,
ruffle his calm vifage by provoking his refentment — I dare fay Mr. Bradford keeps the
Author's account in fuch a regular manner, that
he has no need to fend out for change in order
to balance it — As to his talents and integrity
they foar far above mediocrity and public opinion, though very favourable — Porcupine only
experienced the latter, as he had no opportunity
of forming a juft idea of the former, for, if he
took but a fimple peep into his fenfe-box, he
would not omit taking due notice of it — Mr.
Bradford foon difcovered from the drift of Peter's
converfation, on his return (in fome ungarded
moment), from the temple of the Rofy God
of Wine, that *he had* once *received a fhilling* at
Chatham *to drink his Majefty's health*, when he
enlifted in that divifion (1) — This was a
broad hint, and Bradford (who, we have already
acknowledged, is a foaring genius), took it, and

----

(1). See pag. 24 infin.

honeſtly paid Porcupine, down on the nail, *one ſhilling and ſeven-pence half-penny, Pennſylvania currency* (1), the balance of his obſervations on Doctor Prieſtley's emigration, to enable the ſaid Porcupine · to drink health and fraternity to the American Republic — I judge from the exchange between London and Philadelphia at that period, that Bradford was very accurate in the payment of this balance.

To prove his patriotic *diſpoſition* and anxiety at the ſame time, I ſhall only mention his objections to the firſt production of Porcupine (which he himſelf alfo obſerves), for being not *popular enough*, even to ſave his *windows* (which were in manifeſt *danger*), from total demolition — He expreſſed many other *democratic* fears, which I muſt refer my Reader to in pages 38, 39 and 40 of the famous life, as the detail would be too tedious and pathetic — I cannot, however, paſs over in ſilence one of the moſt ſtriking proofs of his heroic republicaniſm in *his refuſing to ſell* to Porcupine *the copy-right* of his works, *even at the price* he *purchaſed them*, and *though they paſſed through ſeveral editions* (2) —" What! (ſaid our judicious and patriotic Bookſeller behind his counter) ſhall I further encourage
„ this dangerous writer in the ſale of his ariſto-
„ cratic poiſon? No — I ſhall keep them within,
„ leſt they infect the Public like a contagious
„ diſtemper — Should I, even, loſe by them,
„ I have too much of the milk of humanity, and

---

,, the divine nectar of *amor patriæ* in my com-
,, pofition to encreafe my coffers at the expence
,, of my Country " — Were another printer
in his place, Porcupine would not have met
fuch unexpected difappointment, but the caufe
of Republicanifm was the *primum mobile* of this
*fincere democrat* — His zeal, his activity, his cor-
dial wifhes *pro bono publico*, by night and by
day, afleep or awake, rifing, lying, wheezing,
fneezing, p-f-ng, kiffing, f-rt-ng, fnorting, all,
all, entitle him to the general gratitude of the
American People, to whofe refugees during the
war he has been fo tender and charitable, that
they now acknowledge it by inceffant petitions
to Heaven for his future *exaltation*, but not in
the fatal way.

Now, Porcupine, permit me to tell you that
if you regarded your own intereft, you would
ftill employ the prefs of Thomas Bradford Ef-
quire after having received from him (*in notes at
one, two or three months* (1) I fuppofe) the liberal
fum of *four hundred and three dollars, and twenty
one cents* (2); the new coin of the bank of the
United States — You have been too rafh on
the occafion, but be affured that *he will meet you*
(at the court of *Nifi prius*, as I am told) *on fuch
grounds as will convince you that he is not to be tri-
fled with* (3) — I am concerned that fuch a *billet*
fhould have paffed between two fuch good
friends, but it is not, I fear, in my power to re-

---

(1) See pag. 42 in fin.         (3) See the note of Brad-
(2) See pag. 43 in princip. | ford to William Cobbett, pag.
                            ‖ 46 in fin.

concile

concile an englifh Sergeant Major and *honeſt Tom*
the *too, too ſanguine* friend of Democracy — If
*your laugh of about five minutes* (1) has rouſed his
reſentment, I muſt declare to you, that of the two
evils I ſhall always prefer the leſs, and adhere to
the republican (were he even a Braggadocio)
becauſe I love the very ſound; but I can not en-
liſt under his banners who has told us in the beginning of his life, that *he was born in Old England.*

Before I examine, whether Peter has been or
is bribed by Mr. Bond, whom I do not know
but through the channel of our pamphleteer's information, I muſt ſay ſomething of Porcupine's
private diſpoſition. 'Tis a tribute which candor
muſt pay him, and I truſt I ſhall not meet the diſ-
approbation of the Republican Society for unde-
ceiving them, for reconciling oppoſite parties,
and benefiting by the union, by dropping a few
additional pennies in the old worſted ſtocking.

Such is the malice of our democratic news-
paper Writers againſt Peter Porcupine that they
publicly execrate him as an ariſtocrat — Is there
any thing more inconſiſtent than their opinion
on the ſubject? I dare ſay, I can ſilence thoſe fel-
lows in two minutes — Was he not a Republican
and a young britiſh Sans-culotte, when he went
*to the great Hop-Fair at Wey-Hill* and felt an ex-
tatic pleaſure in the toaſt which his father and the
company drank to the health of General Waſh-
ington? (2) Did he not come to this Country

---

(1) See pag. 47 in princip. ‖ . (2) See pag. 16 ad med.

D

with an affurance of enjoying more liberty than
in England ? ( 1 ) Do they fuppofe that after having entertained fuch flattering ideas of the ter-
ritory of the United States, as in page 33 of his
life, he would have come here with any other
political intentions than thofe of unaffected pa-
triotifm ? Did he not fpeak well of the people
of la Vendée, and the Chouans ? — No, no —
Ariftocracy is not his province, or at leaft a private foldier cannot be an ariftocrat.

In page 53 of his life, to evince his patriotic
concern for our Country at the time of the Weftern Infurrection, he ferioufly tells us that *had* he
*been called upon* he *would have ferved too* —
Is not this pure republicanifm ? — I have ftill
more to fay in his favour on the fubject. He
*modeftly* infinuates that *he was not called upon*, but
I have been informed from a *certain* quarter, that
he offered his voluntary fervices as an *officer* to
General Thomas Mifflin, who on his imperfect
relation of military affairs (2) difmiffed him with

---

(1) See pag. 33 in fin.

( 2 ) General Mifflin conceiving, at the time Porcupine
prefented himfelf, that there
would be no immediate oc-
cafion for military aid, indulged a little in his ufual viva-
city after dinner, and having
got fome hint of Peter's military fkill, he afked him what
he judged would be the moft
proper plan to purfue in order to obtain fuccefs in the
expected weftern expedi-

tion — Peter replied with a
low bow in the following
terms " Your Excellency,
" the beft plan you can pur-
" fue is this — Let every
" foldier, pleafe your Ex-
" cellency, carry on his
" fhoulders a rail from our
" country fences, and with
" fuch a quantity of rails
" we will furround all the
" Infurgents together, and
" then, pleafe your Excel-
" lency, with our mufkets,

a very laconic compliment — I muſt ſuppoſe the General only ſkimmed the ſurface of Porcupine's profound knowledge in tactics ; but nevertheleſs his diſintereſted volunteerſhip muſt be held in laſting remembrance by the moſt inveterate democrat — When he modeſtly introduced himſelf as an humble but meritorious man to Governor Mifflin, there were unfortunately two allſeeing Gentlemen preſent, viz : General Stewart (peace to his manes) and Albert Gallatin — The former came there for inſtructions, and the latter about political buſineſs juſt previous to his departure for the weſtern Counties — Mr. Stewart ſeemed prepoſſeſſed in his favour on account of his ſtature, but Gallatin being prejudiced againſt him for ſome *croſs-legged capers* cut in New-York, diſſuaded the Governor from having any thing to do with him — Thus were the budding hopes of Porcupine's military fame in the cauſe of American democracy for ever blaſted by the breath, the deadly breath of a *Genevan !* — In

---

" bayonets &c, we ſhall " compel them to lay down " their pitch-forks, ſhovels, " tongs &c, and, pleaſe " your Excellency, the whole " Inſurrection will be quell- " ed at once " — The General happily ſubduing his riſible powers, obſerved that rails might be cut on the ſpot, where wood is plenty, and by that means we ſhould avoid doing injury to our neighbour and eaſe the fatigue of our brother ſoldier—

" No ( returns the ſergeant major with ſome degree of animation ) pleaſe your Excellency, to cut, ſplit and afterwards form it into rails, is too troubleſome and tedious an employment for a ſoldier, and may probably give an idea of the plan to the enemy — It is better to bring them along with us from hence, if the grand *Pig's pan* may be deemed ſucceſsful ".

fine our cut-throats Jacobins go too far with their conjectures, for they do not underſtand the writings of our Peter at all.

The aſſertion of Porcupine being bribed by a *Britiſh Agent*, is one of the moſt unfounded calumnies that the Argus of New-York and the Aurora of Philadelphia ever publiſhed. The *improbability* of ſuch an aſſertion is evidently demonſtrated by him in the cleareſt manner — He tells us that he *never ſpoke to Mr. Bond but three times* (1), and even from ſo ſhort an acquaintance the Gentleman had taken the liberty of calling him A WILD FELLOW (2) — It is too bad, I declare, that ſuch a reſpectable character ſhould in preſence of others abuſe *a Britiſh Sergeant-Major, after eight years good conduct and ſervice* (3), and after the *thanks given him by General Frederick* (4), merely becauſe *the little iſland of Britain, ſeeming too ſmall a compaſs for him* (5), he came over to America *to enjoy a greater degree of liberty* (6) — Does common ſenſe allow, or can we ſuppoſe that Engliſh Importance will permit, that men bending under the load of opulence and titles will aſſociate with corporals, or ſergeants and pay them *frequent viſits* (7), or can we, with propriety, aſſert that Mr. Bond is attached to the levelling French Equality ?— No, no—There are no ſuch principles in the *ancient, glorious,* and *univerſally admired* Britiſh Conſtitution.

---

(1) See pag. 48 in princip.  | (5) See pag. 20 in princip.
(2) See pag. 50 in princip.  | (6) See pag. 33 in fin.
(3) See pag. 29 in princip.  | (7) See pag. 47 in fin.
(4) See pag. 30 in princip.

But all this is comparatively nothing to the many proofs he can produce of his not being the fuppofed underftrapper or favorite of Mr. Bond — Infinite in number and creditable are the evidences, he can bring forward to *prove the negative.*

When we are affured that the Nobility and Gentry of that Nation in particular, are remarkable for their generofity, can a fober Reader fuppofe, that Mr. Bond fhould be fo near as to *infift on buying* fix fmall pamphlets AT THE WHOLESALE PRICE (1) to fave a few pennies, were it not for his manifeft averfion to the writings of Porcupine, which, it muft be acknowledged, are in toto calculated *to keep alive an attachment to the Conftitution of the United States, and the ineftimable man who is at the head of the Government* (2).

Indeed all the fufpicions fabricated againft him on account of his affection to the Britifh Name (3), are falfe illufions altogether — This attachment of Porcupine ( if my opinion be right ) is an appearance and not a reality — I fincerely believe that his fentiments all flow from the fources of Derifion and Irony, becaufe it cannot be fuppofed, that after having *read fo much* of this Continent, the direful *Theatre of war* for *a long* time, and *the flattering picture given of it by Raynal* (4), his fuperior genius fhould conceive thofe chimerical *prejudices,* which ignorant britifh babies *fuck in with their*

---

(1) See pag. 49 in fin. ‖ (3) See pag. 51 ad med.
(2) See pag. 52 ad med. ‖ (4) See pag. 33 ad med.

*mother's milk* ( 1 ) in favour of their native fpot—
His political enemies, either do not like, or
they are not fufficiently alert in turning corners,
to wind into the labyrinth of the political dupli-
city of our literary champion; hence it is no
wonder if they take Peter Porcupine for
William Cobbett, and William Cobbett for
Peter Porcupine.

I think this will be enough to remove every
doubt of his partial, tho' concealed, adherence
to the republican caufe ; I fhall therefore drop
this fubject on britifh bribery, and anathematife
the fanguinary Democrat, who fhould hereafter
dare to convey any illiberal infinuation to tar-
nifh his fame, or pour the leaft invective o'er
his fine feelings.

On the 23d of July laft we have been fa-
vored with the *Scare-Crow*, on which it is
proper to make fome impartial Obfervations.
While I admired the fruitful invention and
brilliant genius of the Pamphleteer, I really
judged it to be a production haftily ufhered to
the Public as the trumpetting Harbinger of
the famous Life of our Porcupine, juft ready to
be vomited out of the *Blue Shop* oppofite Chrift-
Church, and indeed I could number thoufands
who were of the fame opinion. The ftratagem
of the Author and Printer, was, at the fame
time, happily calculated to excite the curiofity
of our difcerning Citizens, who, undoubtedly,
take pride in ftanding gaping at his windows,
and eyeing his well-ranged Pamphlets which

_____

(1) See pag. 32 in fin.

they buy up at any price he demands. The origin of the letter to the *Kingly* Quaker Friend Oldden has been a problem that could not be folved, even by thofe of his Readers who poffeffed the moft penetration. Some, on the firft perufal, execrated Democracy in the moft bitter terms, and fome endued with the patience of going over the publication again, fhook their heads and grinned cenfure ; feveral, however, who on a third reading had an opportunity of analyzing every fentence, plainly affirmed it to be the lucubration of Honeft Peter infpired by his nightly Grog. This laft opinion feems not unfounded from his own acknowledgment : as our Adventurer then relates that he has been frequently with his father, when he converfed on politics with Martin the Gardener (1), we may readily account for his occafional devotions at the fhrine of Bacchus. I muft, notwithftanding, contradict the affertion refpecting the letter to the Quaker, as it is obvious, at leaft to me, that Porcupine was never guilty of fuch mean catch-penny generalfhip, which I fhall hereafter prove.

But to begin with the feveral obfervations made on the Scare-Crow, while I was prefent, I fhall, in the firft inftance, recite fomé animadverfions on the letter in queftion. " This " Epiftle (faid one) is too flimfy to have been " written by any one but Porcupine. No man " who conveys even fuch fentiments, can be " fo totally ignorant as to conceive that a

(1) See life, pag. 14. in fin,

" Landlord has power to turn his tenant out
" of doors, or hinder him from vending or expo-
" fing for fale what he pleafes, however ridiculous
" and contemptible the commodity; therefore
" the addrefs to frier♩ Oldden was fent by no
" other than he, who wanted a topic for con-
" verfation; and fhould it even have been the
" cafe (continued our obferver) that an afs
" had written fuch a letter, Porcupine fhould
" never have divulged its *falfe orthography* (1)
" to the Reader, in order to lead to a difcovery
" of the Author, but was in decency bound
" to point out where the original could be
" traced, or produce it, if at home, to any one
" who may requeft to fee it. Can the *bad fpell-*
" *ing* of a letter in print, tend more to dif-
" cover the writer than his hand writing? Our
" Pedagogue Cobbett (concluded he) feems
" to be but little acquainted with his *former*
" profeffion, or he has committed an egregious
" and intentional omiffion of his duty which
" muft, of courfe, incline us to think, that he
" aims at betraying the People into the devious
" paths of erroneous conjecture, or concealing
" from them a counterfeit letter written, per-
" haps, with his own hand ".

Another fmiled at his manner of proving the
ariftocratical difpofition of fome of our printers
and Bookfellers, becaufe *Mr. Dobfon and Mr.*
*Carey have printed books on Royal paper, and*
*Mr. Brown has dared to publifh his gazette even*
*on Imperial* (2); " There (faid he) is a Philo-

---

(1) See Scare-Crow, pag. 5. ‖ (2) See Scare-Crow, pag. 16
" fopher

" fopher for you. He even infinuates himfelf
" as a worthy member of our commonwealth
" by faying, that he never abufed our Allies,
" becaufe he never fpoke ill of the *fober* Louis
" the fixteenth and the *chafte* Antoniette ( 1 ).
" Will not the Republicans of Philadelphia
" place his head where the buft of his beloved
" George the fecond refts, to give it the ap-
" pearance of a patriotic relic " ?

But the remark which moft attracted the attention of the hearers, was that relative to his
note in page 21ft of the renowned Scare-Crow.

A decent-looking old Citizen expreffed his
aftonifhment at Porcupine's taking notice of
what he called, *an abominable falfehood*, judicioufly obferving, that an *innocent* perfon would
never regard any grofs calumny, and " whoever
" does ( faid he ), gives room to be fufpected,
" and inftantly converts our ideas of apparent
" calumny into thofe of juft cenfure. Now
" ( continued he ) if Porcurpine denies his
" pilfering, it is a plain proof that the feeming
" falfehood galls him forely, and therefore he
" feels the fmart. His affertion alfo of having
" brought a letter from the American Am-
" baffador at the Hague to Mr. Jefferfon, then
" Secretary of the United States, is a filly
" evafion extremely remote from tending in
" the fmalleft degree to prove, that he had
" not been a fhop-lifter in London. Peter,
" perhaps, might have procured a line from
" that Gentleman through the propitious chan-

( 1 ) See Scare-Crow , page 8 & 9.

E

" nel of petticoat influence. Hence it may be
" inferred, that the moft abandoned vagabond
" might eafily become the time-ferving favo-
" rite of a man in authority, and on that ac-
" count I am not at all furprifed at Porcupi-
" ne's having obtained fuch a boafted, yet
" inglorious, recommendation, which, though
" we fhould allow it to flow from fome other
" fource, has no manner of connection with his
" infamous conduct in London. Of courfe it
" cannot juftify him there; and by infinuating
" nothing in his favor during his ftay among
" the *Cockneighs*, it plainly proves what I
" have before mentioned, that he has been a
" *Shop - Lifter* or *Pick-pocket* in that great
" Metropolis ".

In fpite of my beft exertions to check my
rifible powers, I could not forbear laughing at
the differtation of our venerable orator, who
was, at laft, interrupted by a hickory Quaker
ftanding by the whole time fmoking his fegar,
but fwallowing every word of the paft narrative:
" My Friends, (faid he), let me make a remark
" in time, left I fhould forget it: I remember
" that in the fame note mentioned by our friend
" M. E., Porcupine openly declares that *no*
" *perfon, either in a public or private capacity,*
" *ever called on him twice for the payment of*
" *the fame fum.* Now (continued he) is it to be
" fuppofed that the tax-gatherer, to whom Por-
" cupine alludes, could have the impudence of
" vifiting him again, after having received pay-
" ment? Is there any of us, is there a man
" even in America, who would forget, or pre-
" tend to forget his written receipt in fuch a
" wilful manner? Porcupine acknowledges,

" indeed, the integrity of our tax-gatherer, in
" not calling on him a fecond time after he
" had been paid, but that does not prove
" that the fame tax-gatherer did not wear out
" two pair of fhoes whilft journeying in queft
" of Peter's pence before they were finally paid.
" Our Pamphleteer feems unfettled in his upper
" ftory, and did my toe reach the heel of
" Friend Cobbett, I would tell him to his
" face that he knows nothing about *Lowth's*
" grammar or the mode of expreffing himfelf
" with propriety, though he has been a *School*
" *Mafter* ".

Others produced fatisfactory evidence and
proofs, by which it appeared, that the *Scare-
Crow* was begun three weeks before its publication, and, therefore, could not interfere with the
letter received by John Oldden, unlefs the
Author had the gift of forefeeing on the 29th of
June, what was to happen on the 19th. of July.

To the above pertinent obfervations, a politician juft by me added, that on faturday the
2d. of July, he faw Porcupine coming out of
a *principal* printing-office with a bundle of
old news-papers in his hand, among which he
pointed out to Mr. B—(who was paffing by at
that time), the advertifement of the *Exhibition
in Callow Hill ftreet*(1): " We muft infer from all
" thefe circumftances (obferved he) the previous
" knowledge of Porcupine refpecting the letter
" prefented to John Oldden two weeks after,
" and though I have fome confideration for the
" talents of William Cobbett, the Printer, Book-

_____

(1), See Scare-Crow, pag. 9 & 10.

" feller and Stationer at the Blue Shop oppofite
" Chrift-Church, yet my, friendfhip will never
" induce me to facrifice or conceal the truth.
" He has written and publifhed, however,
(continued Porcupine's admirer with fome
degree of pathos), what he pleafed to write
" and publifh, becaufe the prefs is quite free,
" and if his *Scare-Crow* contains nothing but
" trafh and lies, he certainly has a right
" to print and fell it at an eleven-penny-bit,
" if our generous citizens *do not* grumble at the
" price. Would he have come to America,
" if the Englifh Inquifition had any power
" here ? No, he would have remained at the
" Hague, and carried on a different, and, per-
" haps, more lucrative trade than his dealings
" with Thomas Bradford. After coming here
" to teach us politics, and the arts of civilization
" with unremitting affiduity, the unavailing
" liberty of expofing his maps, charts and blott-
" ing paper to an unmerciful enemy, is but
" a poor reward for his apoftolic labours. It
" is true, that a man of fpirit feldom makes
" fuch a pother as Porcupine did of late,
" but when a defencelefs perfon is in dread
" of a barrel of tar and a feather bed, he fhould
" be prepared for fuch trials by the infliction
" of light punifhments; if not, he muft meet
" his fate like a trembling coward. No, gentle-
" men, (concluded his friend) he is far from
" wifhing to appear as fuch, and if ever the
" Populace inflamed with refentment, fhould
" affemble to annihilate him, they will find him
" as bold as a lion at the Temple of Science
" in fecond ftreet, unlefs fome urgent bufinefs
" fhould call him from home, previous to their

" vifit: fince he quitted France, he carefully
" fhuns all public ceremony and hazardous paf-
" time, fuch as the *Shop-Board, the hempen*
" *Neck-Lace, and Dance in air* ".

Thus paffed on the converfation relative to
our Adventurer, and I would certainly exceed
the limits propofed, were I even to fketch the
various portraits they had drawn of him; but
as I intend to delineate his picture, I muft beg
leave to advance a few impartial hints on the
fubject of this dreadful, villainous, Maratian,
Roberfpierrian, cut-throat, threatening letter —
How do our Democrats mean to difpofe of this
Porcupine? Do they mean to pull down Oldden's
houfe, or lay violent hands on Peter if he happens
to be found? Indeed their fatisfaction would be
trivial, and what is worfe, they would even be
called fanguinary, though they fhould proceed no
further than to tar and feather him a little, without fhedding a fingle drop of his blood. They
may reft affured that he would be no lofer by re-
ceiving fuch treatment, and what would be ftill
more mortifiying to our Sans-culottes, he would
ftart up all at once, like a mufhroom, into confequence, and become more independent in an inftant, than could be expected in a feries of years
by the ordinary courfe of bufinefs. He would
advance every article in his fhop a thoufand per
cent, to be recovered from Congrefs immediately
after his triumphal ride through the City; and as
our great folks are exceedingly prepoffeffed in his
favor, a warrant for money on the Treafury would
be foon flipt into his hands as a compenfation for
all his fufferings. A favorite of Government will
always thrive in fpite of the People, but the public funds muft bleed for his profperity.

Did General N—— lose any thing by having his house burnt by the insurgents in 1794? Not he, indeed — He would never have become a stock-holder in our Banks, were it not for that fortunate circumstance : He was paid three times the value of the property he lost by fire, and he is now a powerful Collector. He pours his choicest blessings on the Excise System, and very justly, for, to it he is indebted for his fortune ; and the only regret he now feels, is, that he had not received a little personal abuse, which would have brought him some thousands more for his damages.

Dear Democrats, you may depend you are deluded in any plans you concert to be avenged of him, for, Porcupine would eternally bark at you, if you attempted to lift the chastening rod. Nay ! If you even flog him to death, his widow would be at you like a spider without a *Cobbett* (I mean a cobweb) and mind that she is a british Heroine, and that is enough to cow the very spirit of Sans-cullotism — In fine, I advise you to take no notice of the well-known intrepidity of our modern Politician, because as sure as you begin to put him to a trial, you will in the end be considered as poltroons — The following anecdote has been related by a reputable Character in Town, relative to Peter.

In Fleet-street, in London, he once insulted an Irish Gentleman, and acted with such insolence as to oblige the enraged Hibernian to kick his a—e, solely through the sinister design of bringing a suit against him and recovering damages, as he did immediately after — It is true that Porcupine was quite destitute of money at that time, for the London Faggots with their fierce blaze soon melt down a Sergeant's purse, and it is probable he may play the same tricks over in America, perhaps, on a more extensive scale — Follow my advice, Citizens, and take no notice of his gasconading, for, either the warmth of your provocked resentment or the guilt of his alarmed conscience, has induced him to cry out murder before-hand, by way of precaution.

I shall conclude these pages by refering my Reader to the particular adventures of Porcupine, which allude to the several Gentlemen whom he has openly attacked in his writings — He will observe that the animosity of our Writer was excited by the insults (whether deserved or undeserved, is a question that Porcupine does not wish to discuss) offered to his person, feelings, and understanding — Had they admired his abilities, respected his honour and praised his immaculate character, no sarcasm or libel would ever have appeared — There is no Author living, and perhaps never will be, possessed of such a disinterested spirit, and solid understanding as our Porcupine — He is incessantly writing for the good of the People, without any pecuniary expectation, but that arising from the sale of his pamphlets, some extra-greasing from *foreign* gentlemen, and a long wished reconciliation with the English Courts of Justice.

If the critics consider his works to be a farrago of nonsense, grammatical errors and bad orthography, there is nothing so extraordinary in all this, as most writers in his sphere are subject to much the same censure — His ideas so croud on

one another, that, for fear of losing them, he dares
not brook the delay of correcting what he writes,
besides he is more inclined to deliver his senti-
ments to the Public in their new-born state,
than in all the glitter of affected phrases and
literary punctilios — The fact is, that he is
certain of the public approbation, for, the People
in general shew themselves very anxious to buy
his performances, were they even blank paper —
I never witnessed a more striking instance of
American generosity in encouraging genius, as
in the very period in which Porcupine commen-
ced business with the date of his future posterity,

Citizens, Porcupine is doing exceedingly
well, and if Luck continues, he will be shortly
enabled to retire, and live on his income. He now
seems quiet, and, for God's sake, do not oblige
him to publish another *Scare-Crow*, for, indeed,
the acids are bad, but vinegar and gall are worse.

POSTSCRIPT.

# POSTSCRIPT

Courteous Reader, I muſt trefpafs on your attention a few minutes longer, and beg leave to inform you, it is my ſincere wiſh that your pleaſure and amuſement in the peruſal of theſe pages may be, at leaſt, adequate to your ex-penſe in purchaſing the pamphlet which contains them — If I am now fortunate enough to attract in ſome degree your kind notice, I ſhall be cheared in the hope of your indulgent patronage to my future labours—Remember, from the preface, that I am a plain good-natured old Batchelor, who *bona fide* has diſcovered the *ſecret* of Porcupine, and it were pity, I declare, to diſappoint me — By your good word to a friend who has not read it, you can render me ſervice, and furniſh him too with more paper than he had before he buys this production. My expectation for the preſent is to get *a new coat upon my back* without reſorting to our *charitable patriot* and printer Thomas Bradford Eſquire, for, indeed, the habit I daily wear is almoſt broken out at the elbows.

Another thing I muſt obſerve to you, is, that the *lending* of a pamphlet from one friend to another is now a days conſidered ungenerous in the lender, and ſtingy in the borrower, and both, tho' they purſue different ways, contribute to check the flights of ſoaring genius — I hope you will indulge my bluſhing, for I am rather modeſt, and from this hint you will be

F.

good enough to defire every applicant to gra-
tify his curiofity at his own expenfe.

I do not know what Mr. Bond will call me
hereafter, I hope nothing worfe than *Wild*
*Fellow* — At any rate he muft not think to
purchafe at a *wholefale price*, for I have made
it a point (as the fame allowance that Thomas
Bradford has made, can not be expected from
me) to fell *by Retail*, which I deem the moft
advantageous mode of proceeding for Authors
in my humble fphere.

It will be alfo neceffary to remind you, kind
Reader (I mean to addrefs the quill-driver) that
in cafe you have determined to follow the fame
career I have taken, I fhall by no means be
jealous, provided you fhew yourfelf a better
fellow, or, at leaft, equal to Quickfilver; if
not, I fhall not fuffer you to introduce your
catch-pennies without taking fome fharp notice
of you, left my cuftomers fhould be difappointed.
I underftand that an anfwer to the Life of
Porcupine will fhortly be publifhed from a fecret
quarter, and indeed I fufpect that it is by you,
Mr. Sim. Sansculotte, who wifhes to cut more
capers with another *Roafter* — Do you believe
that in order to *check* any *progrefs of political
blafphemy*, it is neceffary to introduce Maciver's
fcience on cookery? — However fkilful you
may be in that profeffion, I requeft you to
confider that the prefent feafon is too hot, and
will not permit you, on account of your hafty
conftitution, to overheat yourfelf without the
moft dangerous confequences — If you cool
yourfelf, you'll eafily perceive that there is no
neceffity of proftituting the Caufe you intend

to vindicate, by anſwering William Cobbett in
equally as blackguard a ſtyle as his—However,
I ſhall ſee your production, if it comes out —
I hope it will poſſeſs far ſuperior merit to my
preſent one, and if ſo, I ſhall not heſitate a moment to give up the ground — If otherwiſe,
would you not do the ſame? I have reaſon to
expect it, if you ſtick to your colours, for, you
will allow, that it is diſagreeable to ſee a fair
engagement interrupted by greaſy jacks, pots,
and frying-pans. Only, think and reſolve.

Finally, my good friend, I addreſs you with
candor — and why not? Do you want a humorous Writer? — I am your man — I am
not ſo aſpiring as Porcupine, who will be no
body's buffoon — I will be yours and his alſo,
if he pleaſes to honour me with ſuch an employment — Do you want to kick up a literary
duſt between us? — I am ready for it — I'll
have at Peter Porcupine like a good fellow,
and you ſhall, then, ſee more fun than
you expect — I will write (and indeed you
may compute from the ſhort ſpace of time this
publication has been in hands (1) ) more

---

(1) Porcupine publiſhed
his life and adventures on the
8th inſtant, and this pamphlet
was completely finiſhed and
a correct copy drawn on the
17th when it was put to
preſs; yet, it muſt be obſerved that from nine in the
morning till ſeven in the
evening, it was not in the
power of the Author to de-
vote any attention to it, on
account of his daily employment — Had he the whole
day to himſelf, how many
*Bones to gnaw for the* Ariſtocrats could he write in a
month's time? Should ſuch
*happy days* come, he will not
be cenſured (it is expected)
for entertaining *an honeſt
pride*, over, and above our
*Britiſh ſergeant major.*

in a day than he is able in one week, and (by your permiſſion) with a little more ſenſe; and it ſhall alſo appear, that my ſcribbling will be equal to our Hiſtorian's *wit* againſt Mr. Swan-wick — What more do you want of me ? — I am fit for every thing, except the *noĉturnal ſcenes* of Porcupine — Buy my pamphlets, that's all I require, and you ſhall ſee what you do not now ſee, a *bull tamed.*

To conclude (ſhould I get the *new coat* as afore-ſaid),'in three weeks from this date, I will publiſh a Comedy on the *tranſaĉtions* of Peter Porcupine in London, as before glanced in page 10 and 23 of this Work, and I pledge my honour that it will be as *intereſting, inſtruĉtive* and *humorous* Production as you could expect on the ſubjeĉt— Its title will be as follows :

THE

# DISAPPOINTMENT

O R

## PETER PORCUPINE IN LONDON,

A

### COMEDY IN THREE ACTS

WRITTEN BY

## JAMES QUICKSILVER.